THE Baby's handbook

with over 20 songs that every kid should know

by Dayna Martin

ENGAGE BOOKS
VANCOUVER

1

A MESSAGE FROM THE PUBLISHER

These 21 nursery rhymes are sung in households around the world. While we have done our best to present these songs, everyone has their own special way of singing each nursery rhyme. We encourage you to keep singing the version of each rhyme that feels best to you. The main purpose of these rhymes is to engage your baby through sight and sound.

A.R. Roumanis

ENGAGE BOOKS

Mailing address
PO BOX 4608
Main Station Terminal
349 West Georgia Street
Vancouver, BC
Canada, V6B 4A1

www.engagebooks.ca

Written & compiled by: Dayna Martin
Edited & designed by: A.R. Roumanis
Photos supplied by: Shutterstock
Photo on page 47 by: Faye Cornish

FIRST EDITION / FIRST PRINTING

LIBRARY AND ARCHIVES CANADA CATALOGUING IN PUBLICATION

Martin, Dayna, 1983–, author
    The baby's handbook : 21 black and white nursery rhyme songs : Itsy bitsy spider, Old MacDonald, Pat-a-cake, Twinkle twinkle, Rock-a-by baby, and more / Dayna Martin ; A. R. Roumanis, editor.

Issued in print and electronic formats.
ISBN 978-1-77226-333-6 (bound). –
ISBN 978-1-77226-334-3 (paperback). –
ISBN 978-1-77226-335-0 (pdf). –
ISBN 978-1-77226-336-7 (epub). –
ISBN 978-1-77226-337-4 (kindle)

1. Nursery rhymes, English.
I. Roumanis, A. R., editor
II. Title.
III. Title: Twenty one black and white nursery rhyme songs.

PZ8.3.M375BA 2017   J398.8   C2017-902655-0
                                        C2017-902656-9

ITSY BITSY 4

DIDDLE 6

MULBERRY 8

TEA POT 10

BUMBLE BEE 12

DUKE OF YORK 14

BANBURRY 16

PAT-A-CAKE 18

LITTLE LAMB 20

MUFFIN MAN 22

THE GARDEN 24

RING AROUND 26

MACDONALD 30

TWINKLE 36

HICKORY 38

ROCK-A-BY 44 3

The itsy bitsy spider
Climbed up the waterspout.
Down came the rain
And washed the spider out.

Out came the Sun
And dried up all the rain.
And the itsy bitsy spider
Climbed up the spout again.

5

Hey diddle diddle,
The cat and the fiddle,
The cow jumped over the Moon.

6

The little dog laughed,
To see such craft,
And the dish ran away
with the spoon.

All around the mulberry bush,
The monkey chased the weasel.
The monkey thought
It was all in good fun,
Pop! goes the weasel.

8

A penny for a spool of thread,
A penny for a needle—
That's the way the money goes,
Pop! goes the weasel.

9

I'm a little tea pot short and stout,
Here is my handle, here is my spout.

When I get all steamed up
Hear me shout!
Tip me over and poor me out.

Hickety pickety bumble bee,
Won't you say your name for me?
Hickety picket bumble bee,
Can you spell your name for me?

12

Hickety picket bumble bee,
Can you clap your name for me?
Hickety picket bumble bee,
Can you whisper your name for me?

The grand old Duke of York,
He had ten thousand men;
He marched them up
To the top of the hill,
And he marched them down again.

14

And when they're up, they're up,
And when they're down, they're down,
And when they're only half-way up,
They were neither up nor down. 15

Ride a cock-horse
To Banbury Cross.
To see a fine lady
Upon a white horse.

16

Rings on her fingers
And bells on her toes.
And she shall have music
Wherever she goes.

Pat-a-cake, pat-a-cake, baker's man.
Bake me a cake as fast as you can.

18

Pat it, and roll it,
And mark it with a "B".
And put it in the oven,
For baby and me!

Mary had a little lamb,
Little lamb, little lamb,
Mary had a little lamb,
Whose fleece was white as snow.

And everywhere that Mary went,
Mary went, Mary went,
Everywhere that Mary went,
The lamb was sure to go.

21

Do you know the muffin man,
The muffin man, the muffin man,
Do you know the muffin man,
Who lives in Mulberry Lane?

Yes I know the muffin man,
The muffin man, the muffin man,
Yes, I know the muffin man,
Who lives in Mulberry Lane.

Round and round the garden,
Like a teddy bear.

One step, two step,
Tickle you under there.

Ring-a-round the rosie,
A pocket full of posies,

Husha! Husha!
We all fall down.

There was a man who lived in the moon,
Lived in the moon, lived in the moon.
There was a man who lived in the moon,
And his name was Aiken Drum!

28

And he played upon a ladle,
A ladle, a ladle.
And he played upon a ladle,
And his name was Aiken Drum!

29

Old MacDonald had a farm,
E-I-E-I-O.
And on his farm he had a cow,
E-I-E-I-O.
With a "moo-moo" here,
And a "moo-moo" there.

Here a "moo" there a "moo"
Everywhere a "moo-moo."
Old MacDonald had a farm,
E-I-E-I-O.

Row, row, row your boat,
Gently down the stream.
Merrily, merrily, merrily, merrily,
Life is but a dream.

Baa, baa, black sheep,
Have you any wool?
Yes, sir, yes, sir,
Three bags full.

One for the master,
And one for the dame,
And one for the little boy
Who lives down the lane.

Twinkle, twinkle, little star,
How I wonder what you are!
Up above the world so high,
Like a diamond in the sky.

As your bright and tiny spark,
Lights the traveller in the dark,
Though I know not what you are,
Twinkle, twinkle, little star.

Hickory, dickory, dock.
The mouse ran up the clock.

The clock struck one,
The mouse ran down,
Hickory, dickory, dock.

39

Star light, star bright,
The first star I see tonight;

I wish I may, I wish I might,
Have the wish I wish tonight.

I've been working on the railroad,
All the live-long day.
I've been working on the railroad,
Just to pass the time away.

Can't you hear the whistle blowing,
Rise up so early in the morn;
Can't you hear the captain shouting,
"Dinah, blow your horn!"

Rock-a-bye baby,
On the treetop.
When the wind blows,
The cradle will rock.

When the bough breaks,
The cradle will fall.
And down will come baby,
Cradle and all.

THE Baby's handbook

activity

Match the following nursery rhyme characters to the pictures below. Can you find **Mary's Lamb, Twinkle Twinkle, Little Teapot, Hickety Pickety Bumble Bee, Teddy Bear, Muffin Man, Monkey, Itsy Bitsy Spider,** and the **Cow** jumping over the **Moon?**

Answer: Mary's Lamb

Answer: Twinkle Twinkle

Answer: Little Teapot

Answer: Monkey

Answer: The Cow jumping over the Moon

Answer: Teddy Bear

Answer: Muffin Man

Answer: Itsy Bitsy Spider

Answer: Hickety Pickety Bumble Bee

Find more early concept books at www.engagebooks.ca

About the Author

Dayna Martin is the mother of three young boys. When she finished writing *The Toddler's Handbook* her oldest son was 18 months old, and she had newborn twins. Following the successful launch of her first book, Dayna began work on *The Baby's Handbook, The Preschooler's Handbook,* and *The Kindergartener's Handbook.* The ideas in her books were inspired by her search to find better ways to teach her children. The concepts were vetted by numerous educators in different grade levels. Dayna is a stay-at-home mom, and is passionate about teaching her children in innovative ways. Her experiences have inspired her to create resources to help other families. With thousands of copies sold, her books have already become a staple learning source for many children around the world.

Translations

ENGLISH / SPANISH

ENGLISH / FRENCH

ENGLISH / GERMAN

ENGLISH / MANDARIN

ENGLISH / ITALIAN

ENGLISH / GREEK

and many more...

Looking for a different translation?
Contact us at: alexis@engagebooks.ca
with your ideas.

 Show us how you enjoy your **#handbook**. Tweet a picture to **@engagebooks** for a chance to win free prizes.

CPSIA information can be obtained
at www.ICGtesting.com
Printed in the USA
BVOW05s1440071217
502143BV00021B/650/P